the AMAZING SPIDER-MAN™

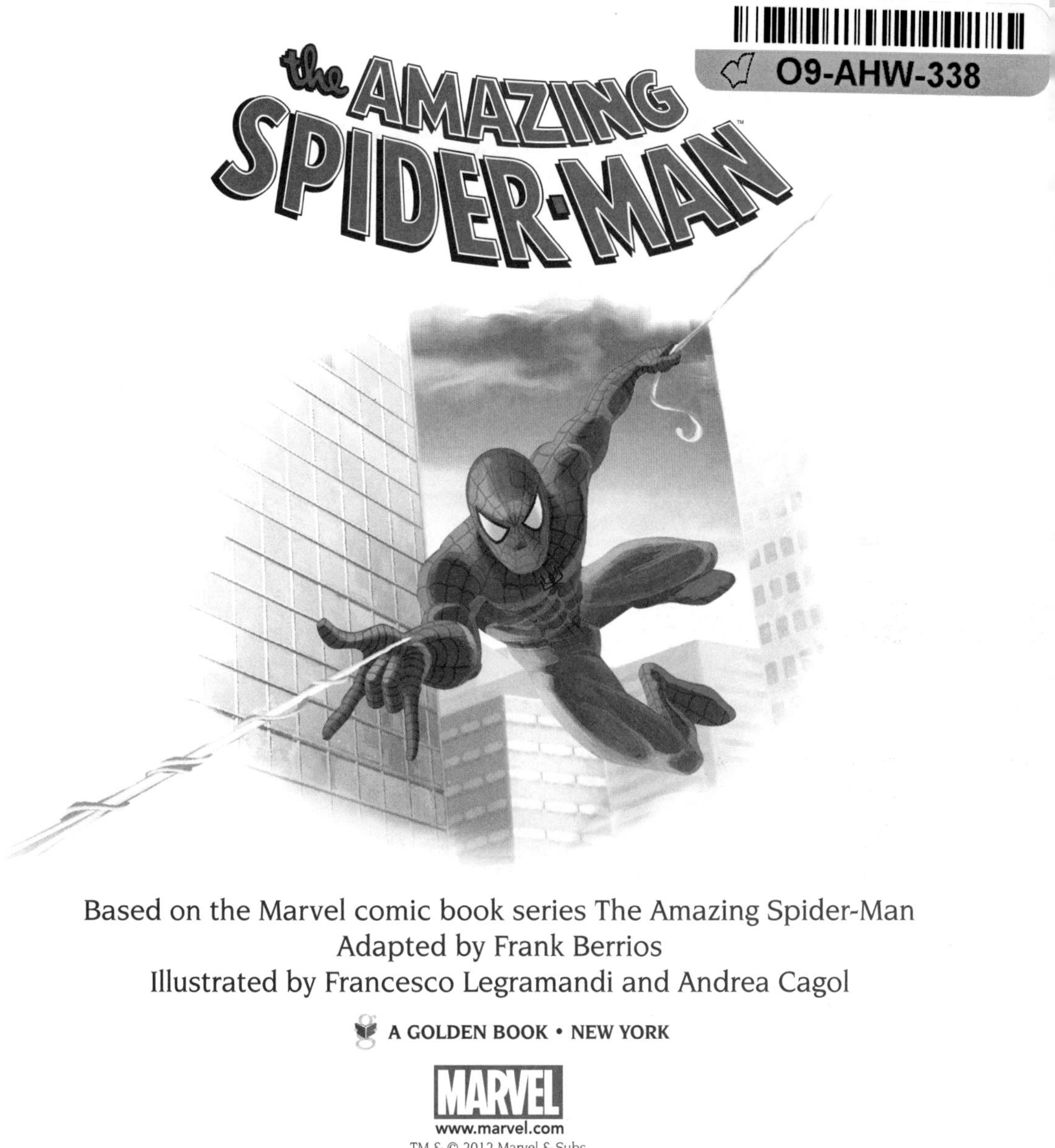

Based on the Marvel comic book series The Amazing Spider-Man
Adapted by Frank Berrios
Illustrated by Francesco Legramandi and Andrea Cagol

A GOLDEN BOOK • NEW YORK

MARVEL
www.marvel.com

Published in the United States by Golden Books, an imprint of Random House Children's Books, a division of Random House, Inc., 1745 Broadway, New York, NY 10019, and in Canada by Random House of Canada Limited, Toronto. Golden Books, A Golden Book, A Little Golden Book, the G colophon, and the distinctive gold spine are registered trademarks of Random House, Inc.
randomhouse.com/kids
ISBN: 978-0-307-93107-8
Printed in the United States of America
10 9 8 7 6

Peter Parker was once an ordinary teenager—
until he was bitten by a **radioactive spider**!

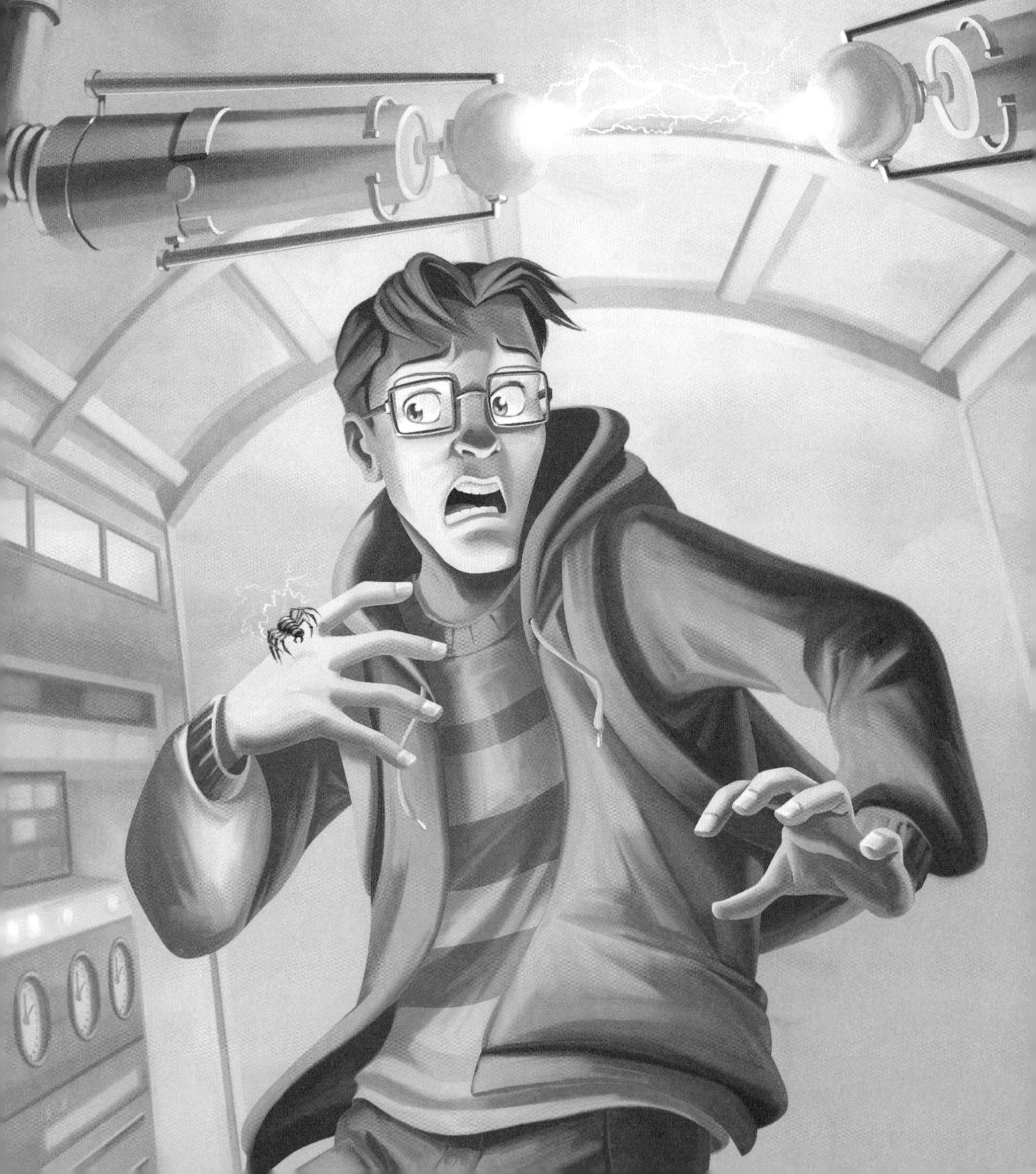

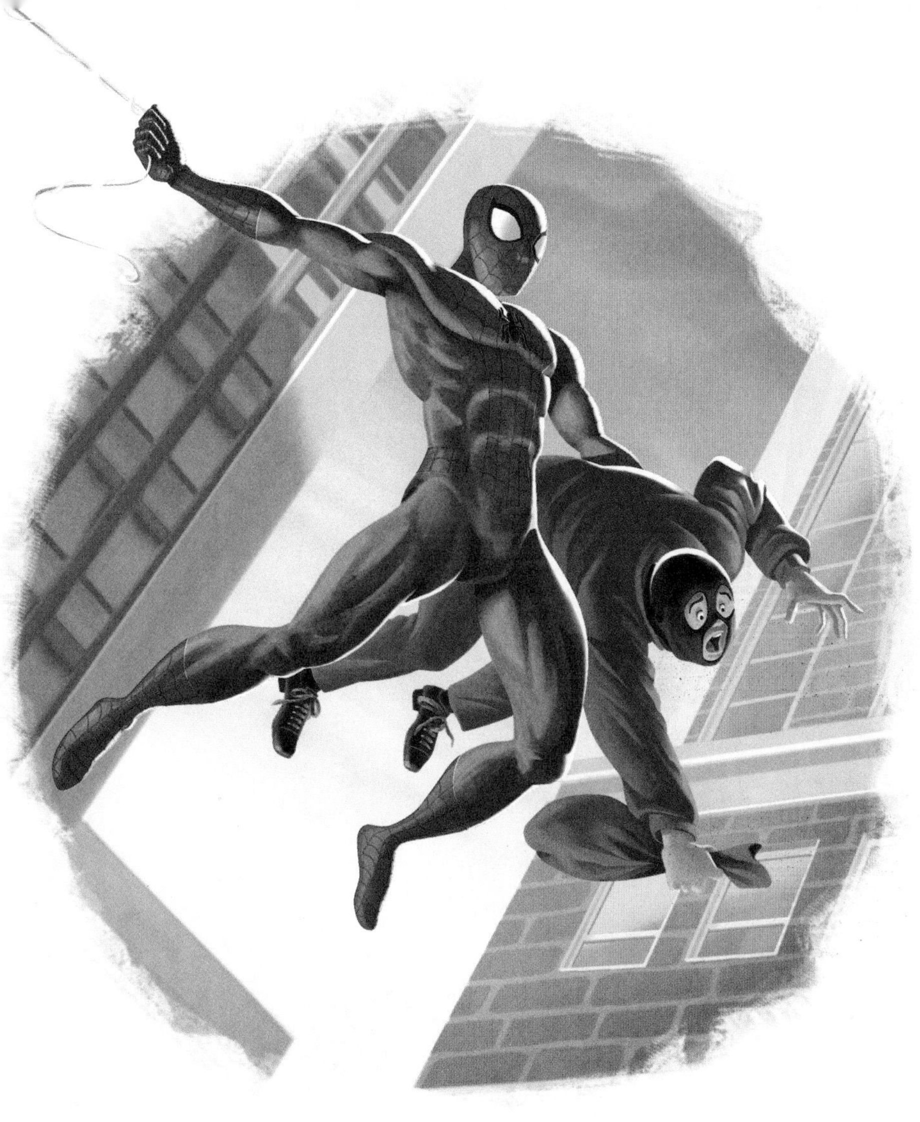

The bite gave Peter super strength and the amazing ability to cling to walls—just like a man-sized spider. So Peter Parker decided to become the super hero called **Spider-Man**!

Peter Parker created a costume to wear so that no one would know he was really Spider-Man.

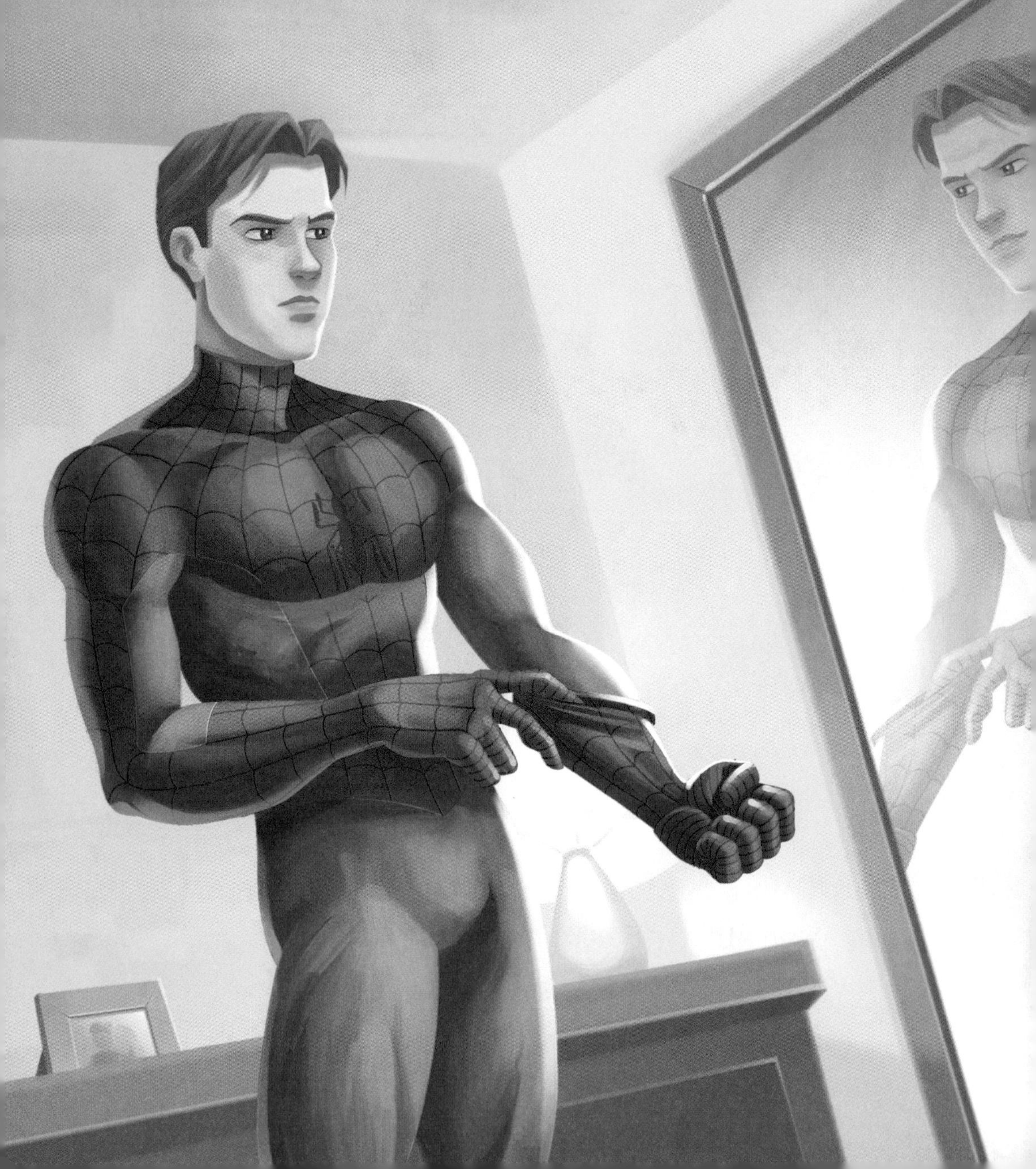

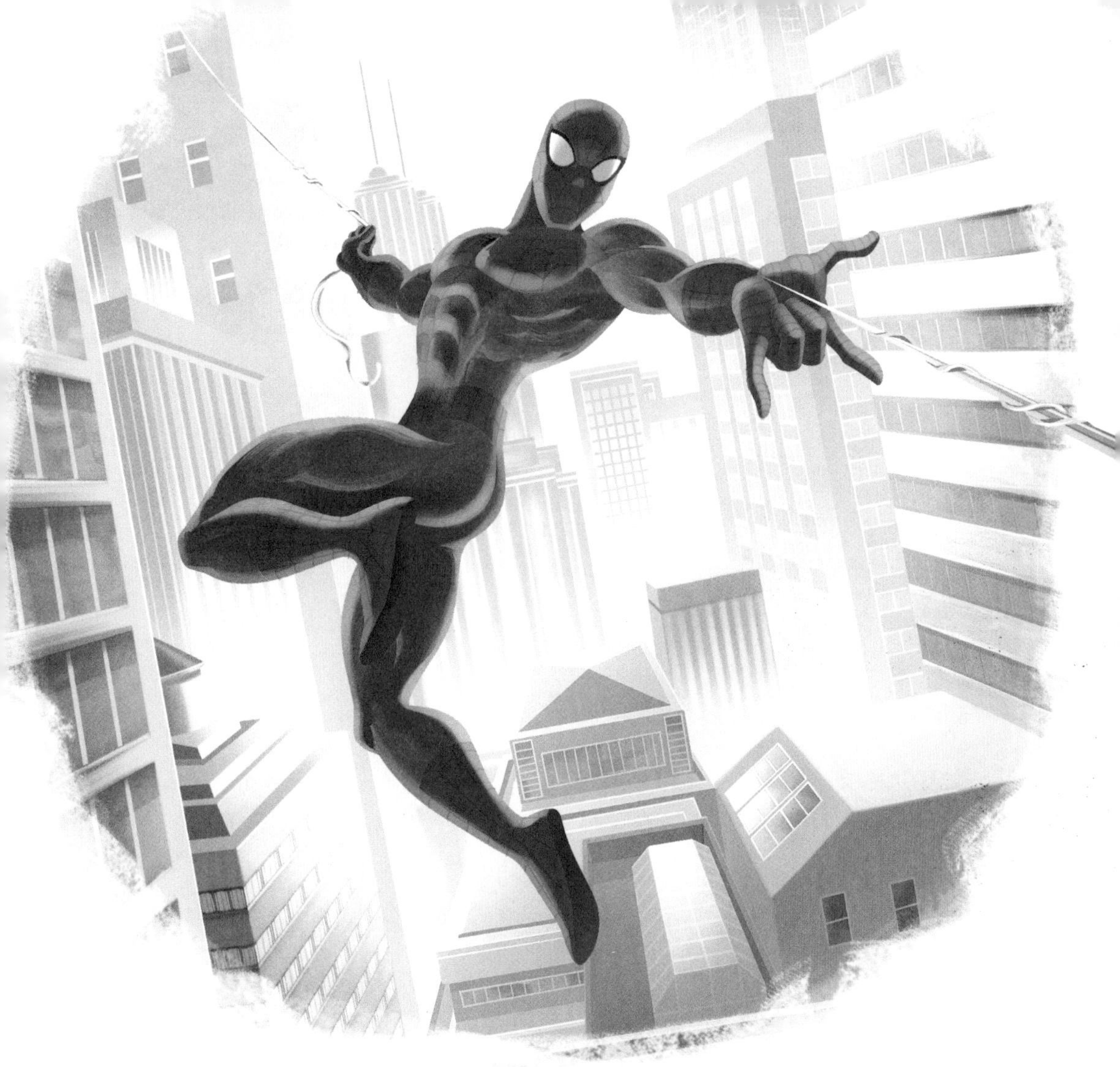

Peter also invented **web shooters** that allowed him to swing through the city from building to building.

Spider-Man can use his web shooters in many ways.

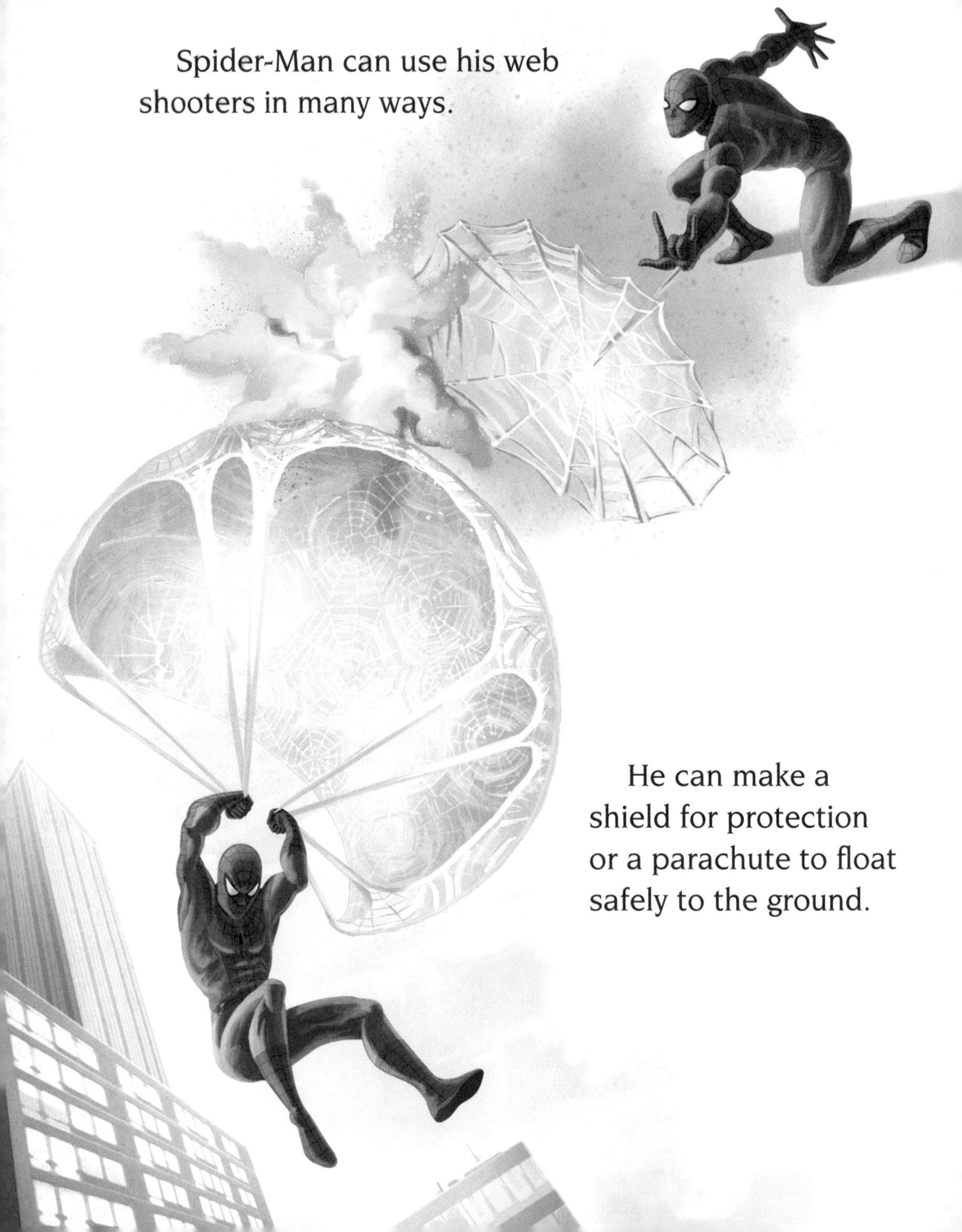

He can make a shield for protection or a parachute to float safely to the ground.

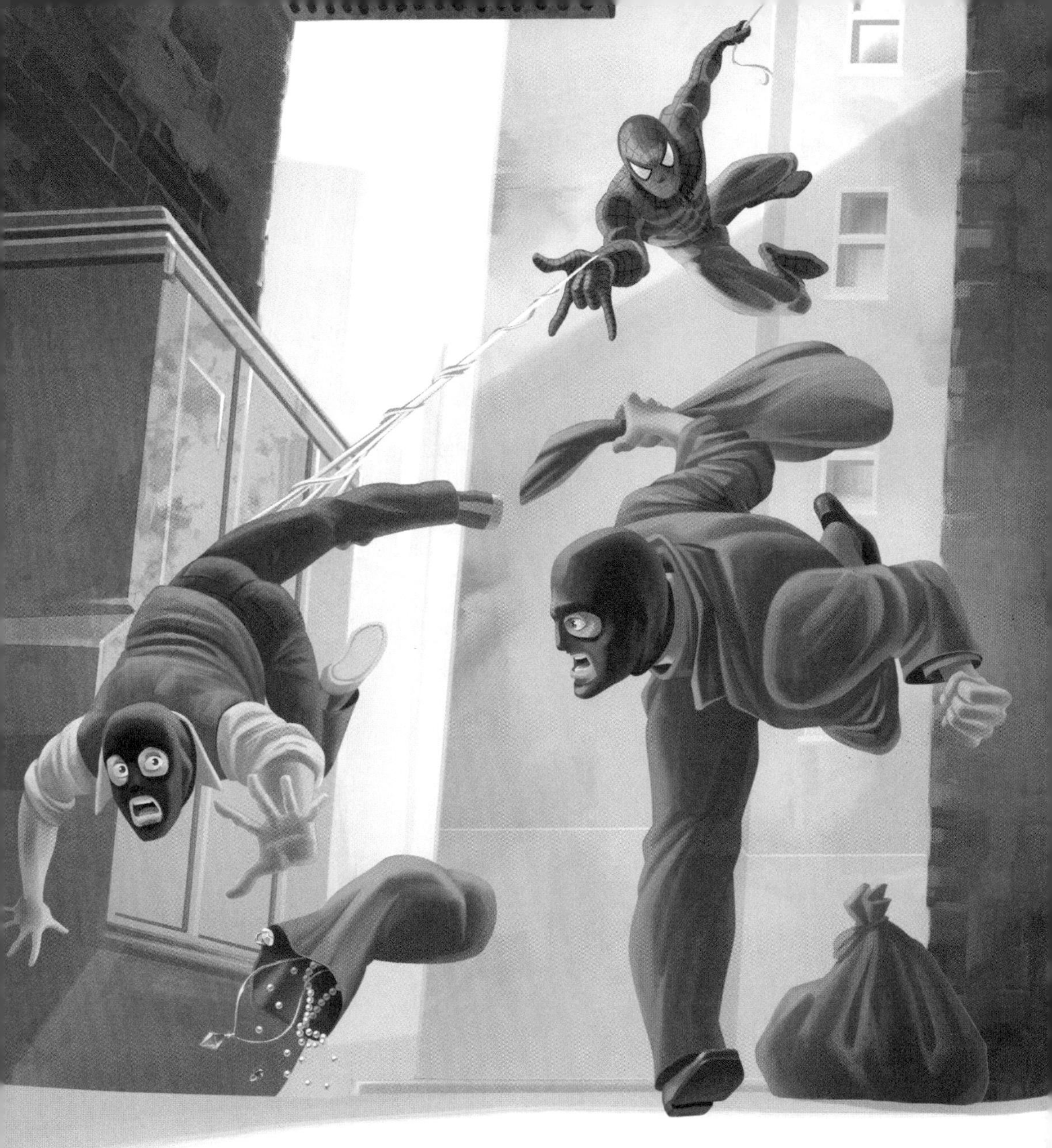

And Spider-Man can use his webs to stop bad guys in their tracks!

Spider-Man also has a "spider sense," which alerts him to danger. When his **spidey-sense** starts tingling, Spider-Man knows that trouble is nearby!

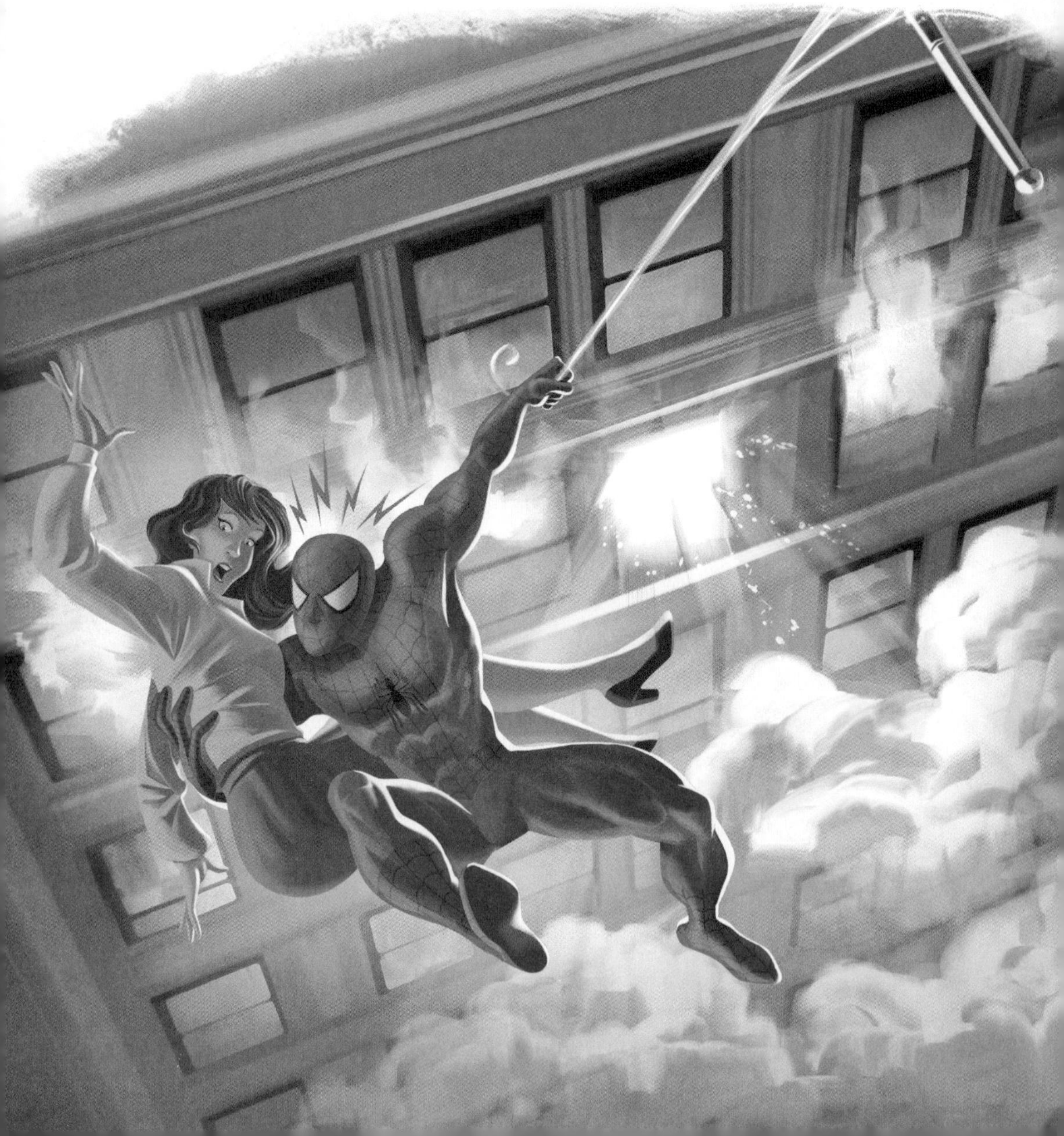

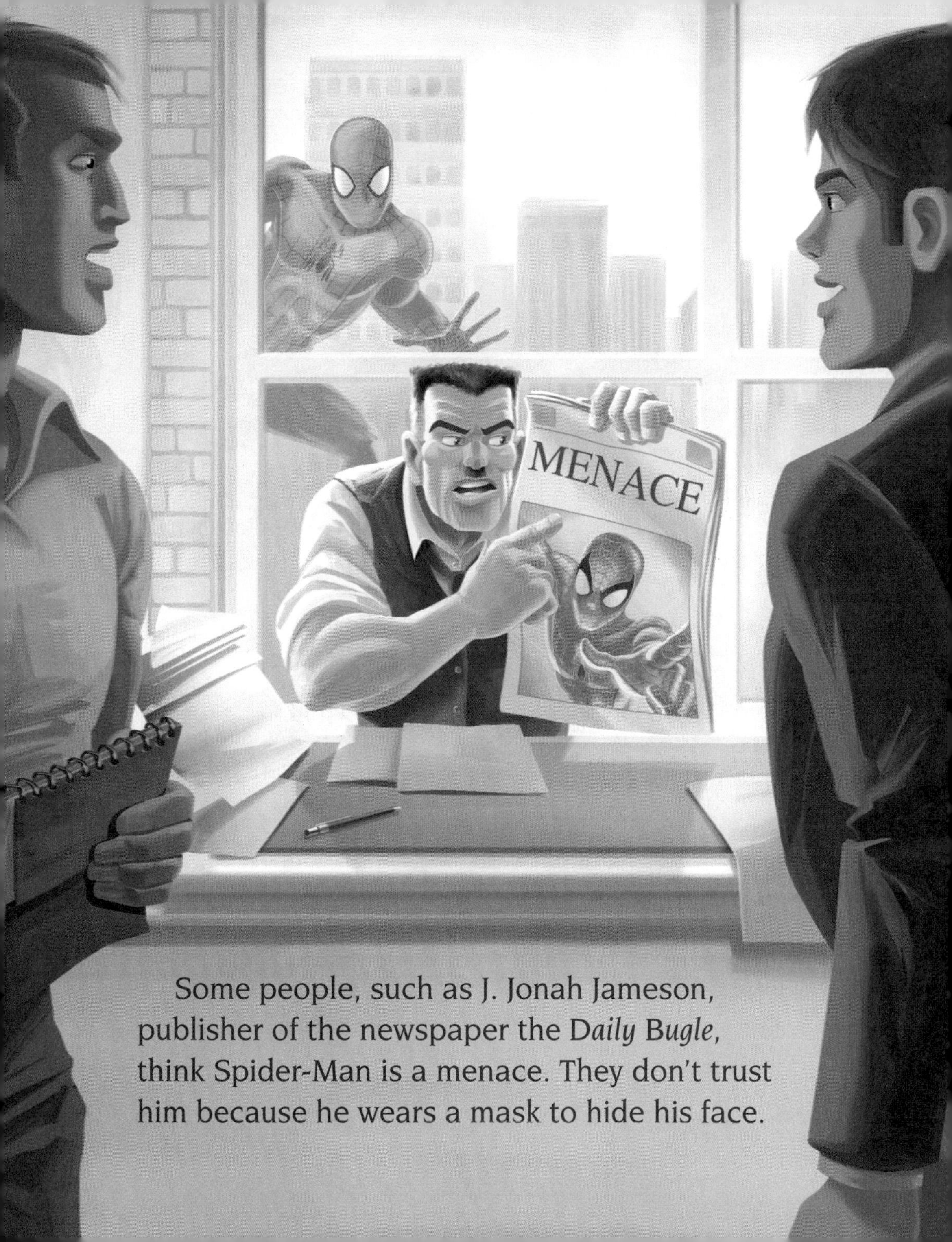
MENACE

Some people, such as J. Jonah Jameson, publisher of the newspaper the *Daily Bugle*, think Spider-Man is a menace. They don't trust him because he wears a mask to hide his face.

But most people know that Spider-Man is really a **hero**!

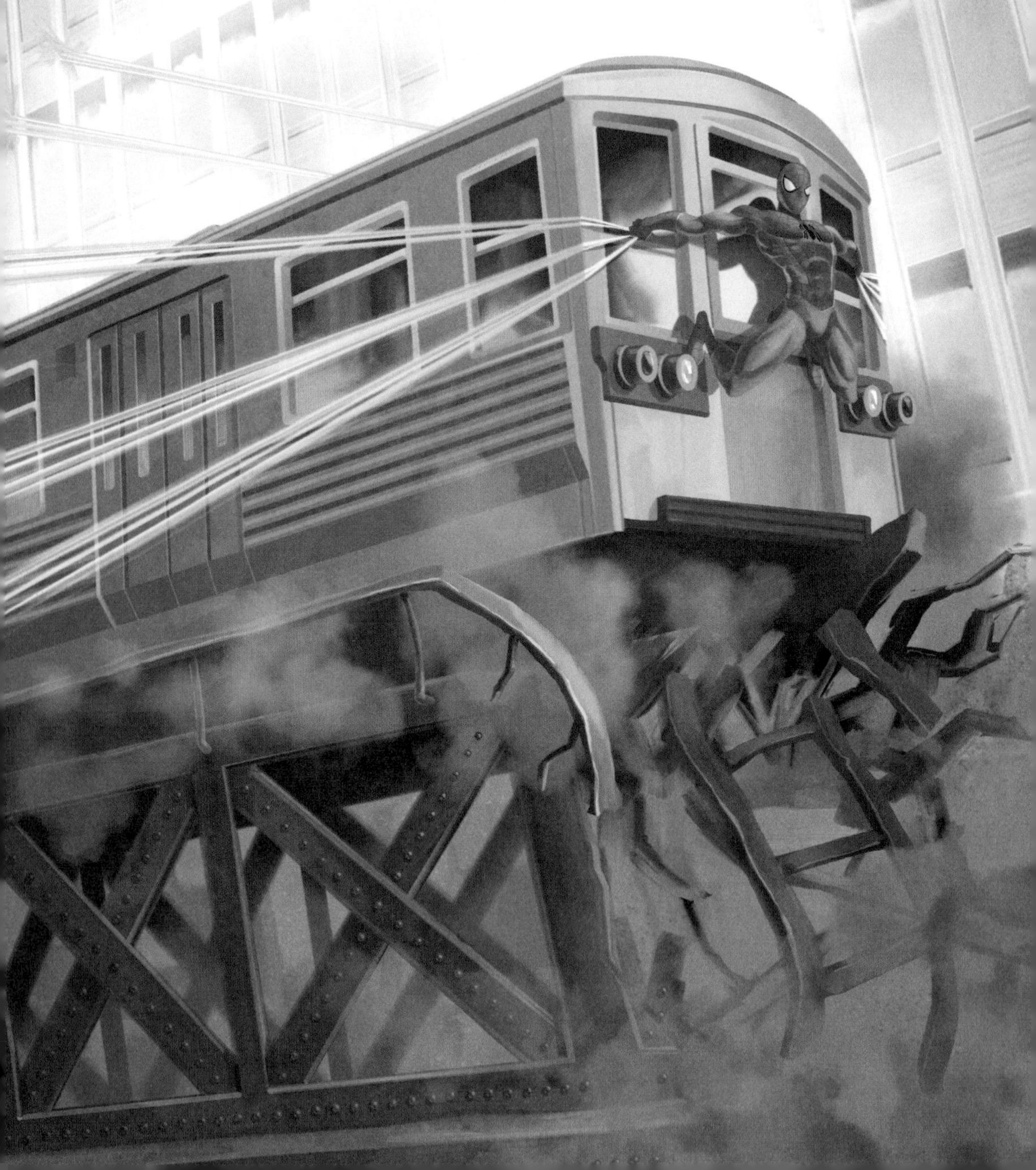

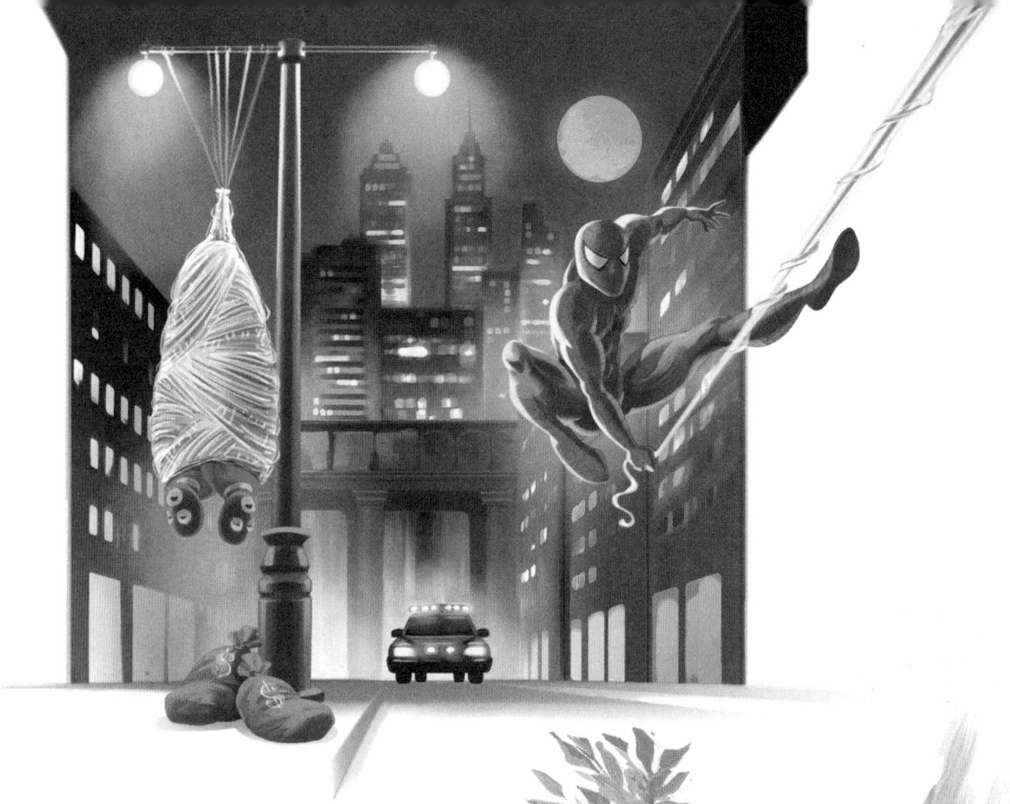

No trouble is too big—or too small—for Spider-Man to handle!

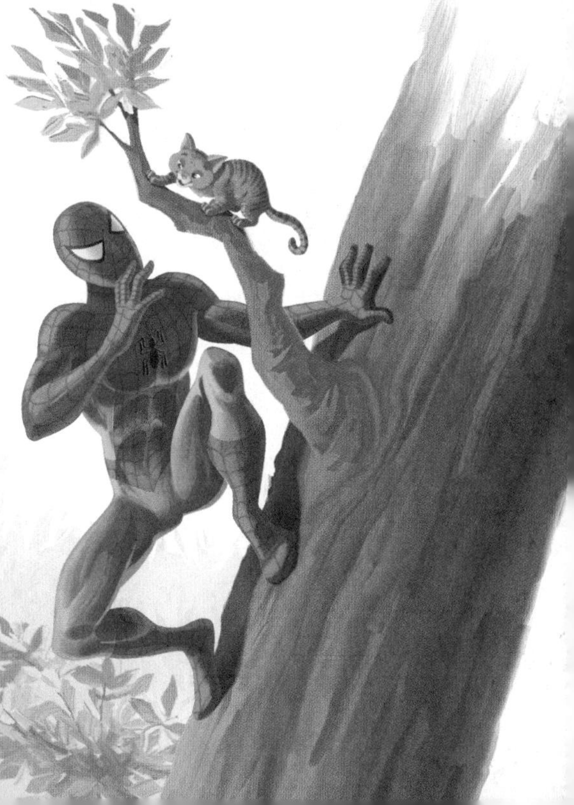

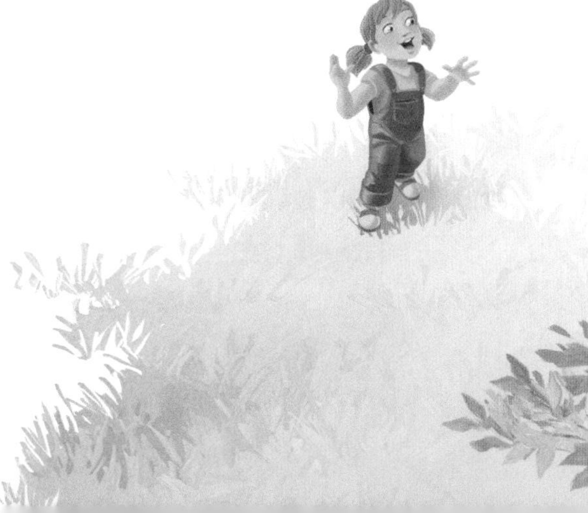

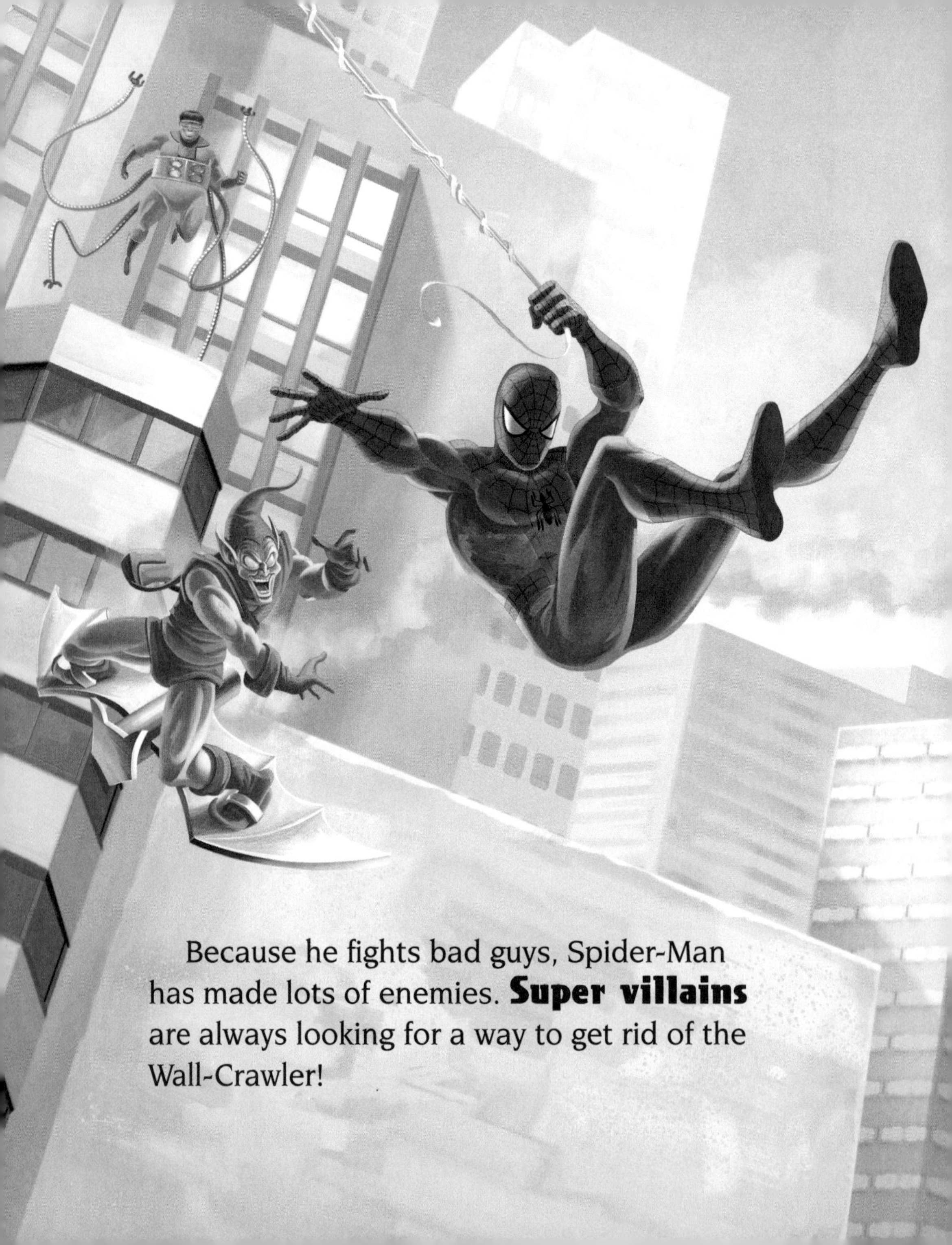

Because he fights bad guys, Spider-Man has made lots of enemies. **Super villains** are always looking for a way to get rid of the Wall-Crawler!

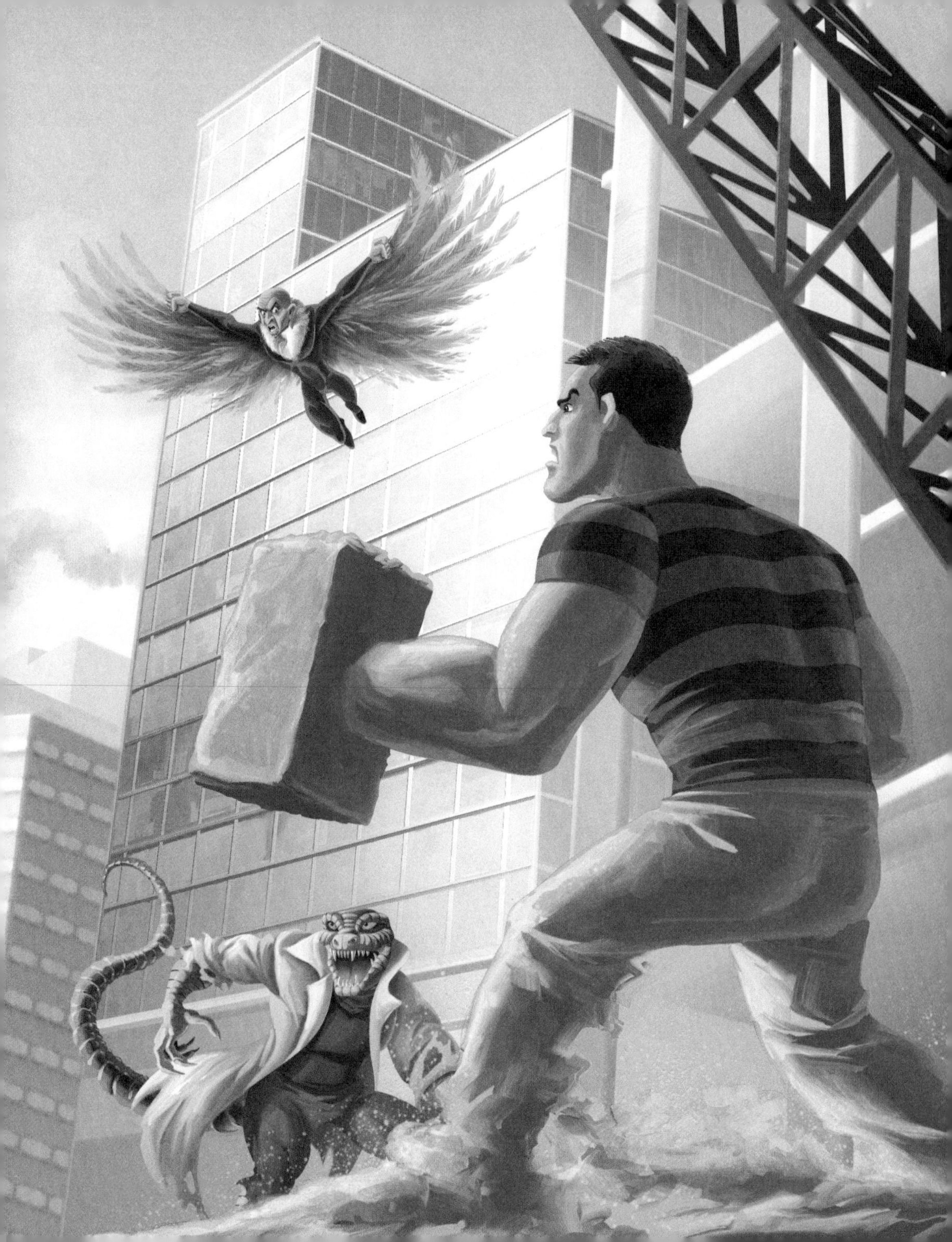

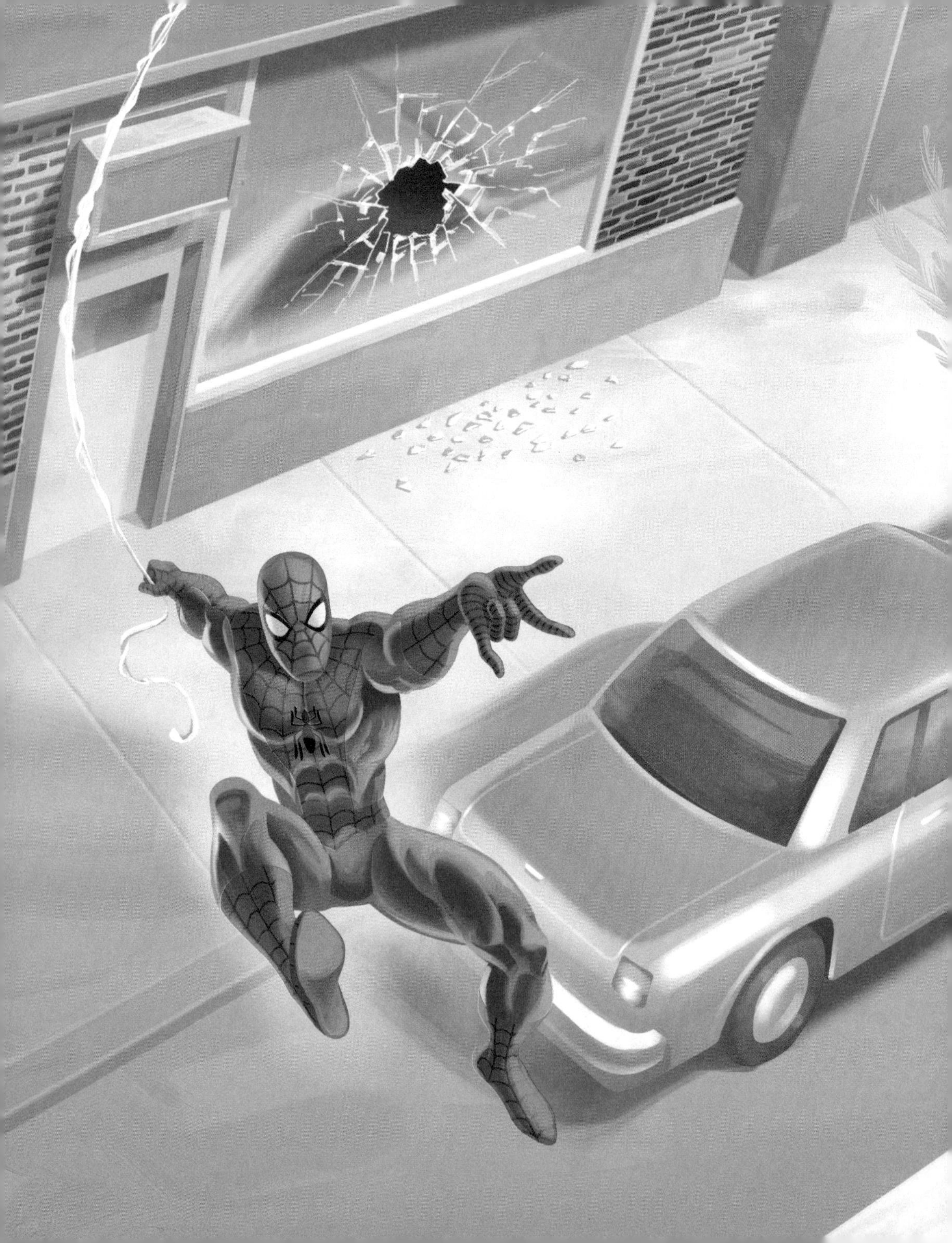

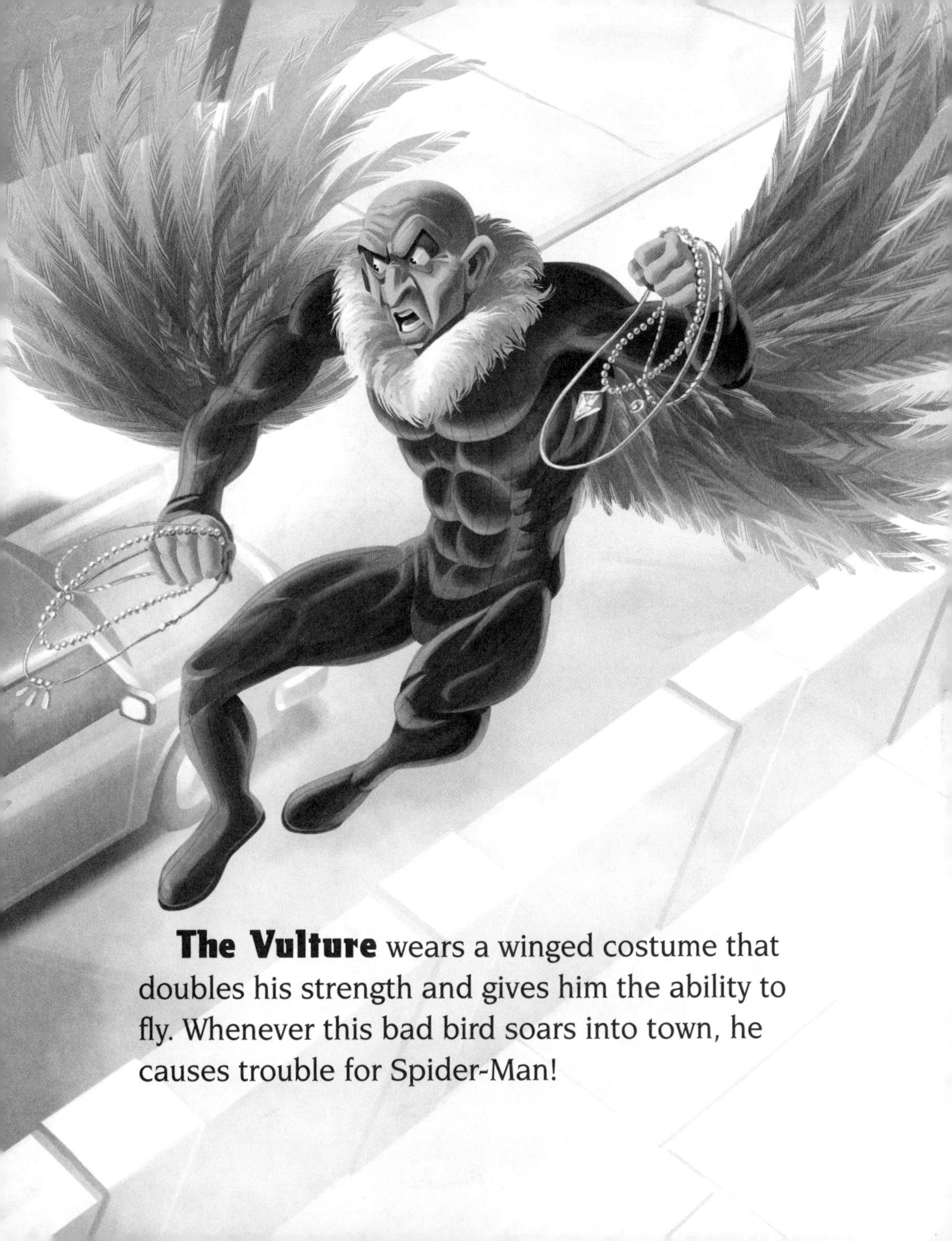

The Vulture wears a winged costume that doubles his strength and gives him the ability to fly. Whenever this bad bird soars into town, he causes trouble for Spider-Man!

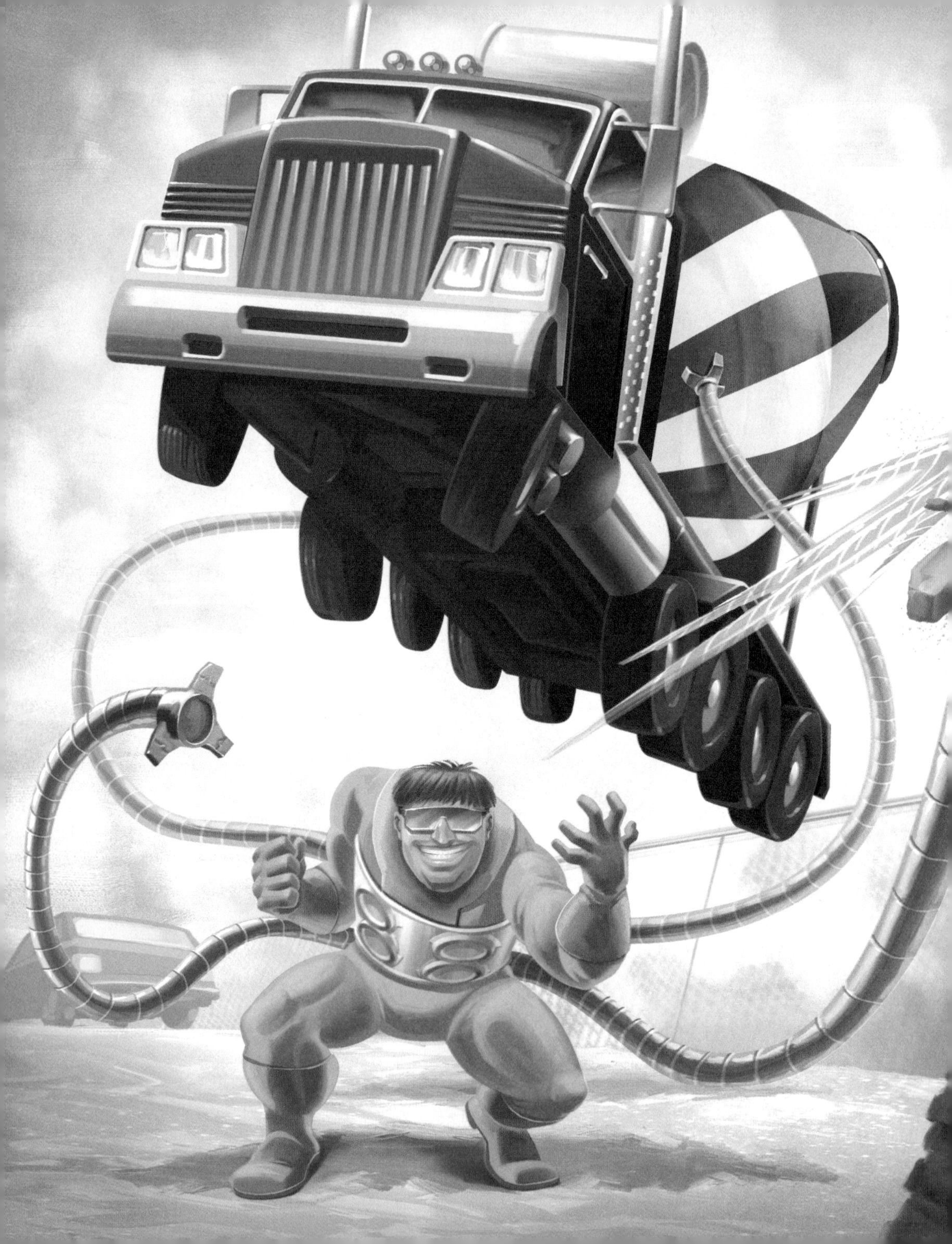

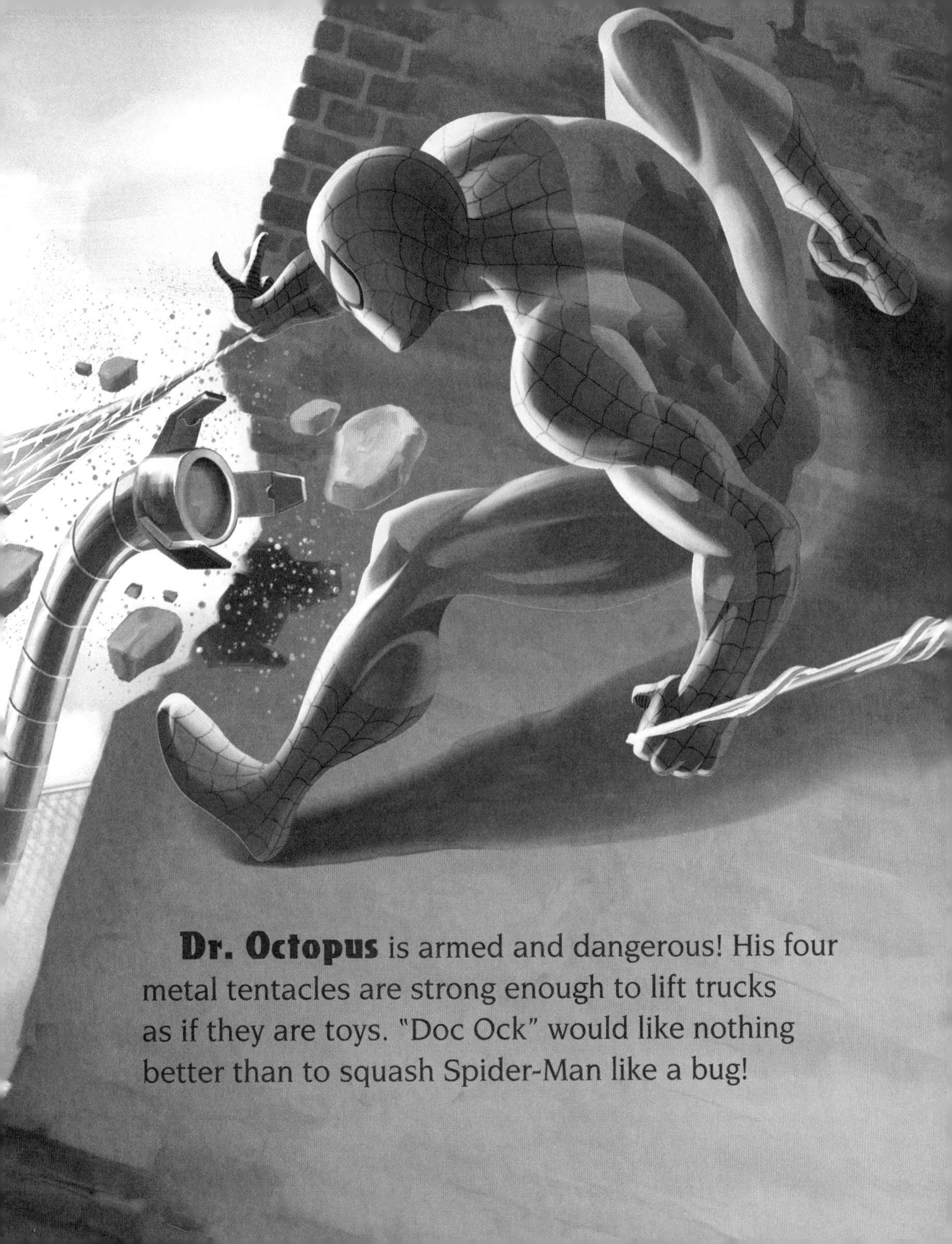

Dr. Octopus is armed and dangerous! His four metal tentacles are strong enough to lift trucks as if they are toys. "Doc Ock" would like nothing better than to squash Spider-Man like a bug!

The Sandman is made of living sand! He can slip through the smallest cracks or make his fist rock-hard to smash his enemies. But Spider-Man thinks fast and always cleans the floor with this gritty thug!

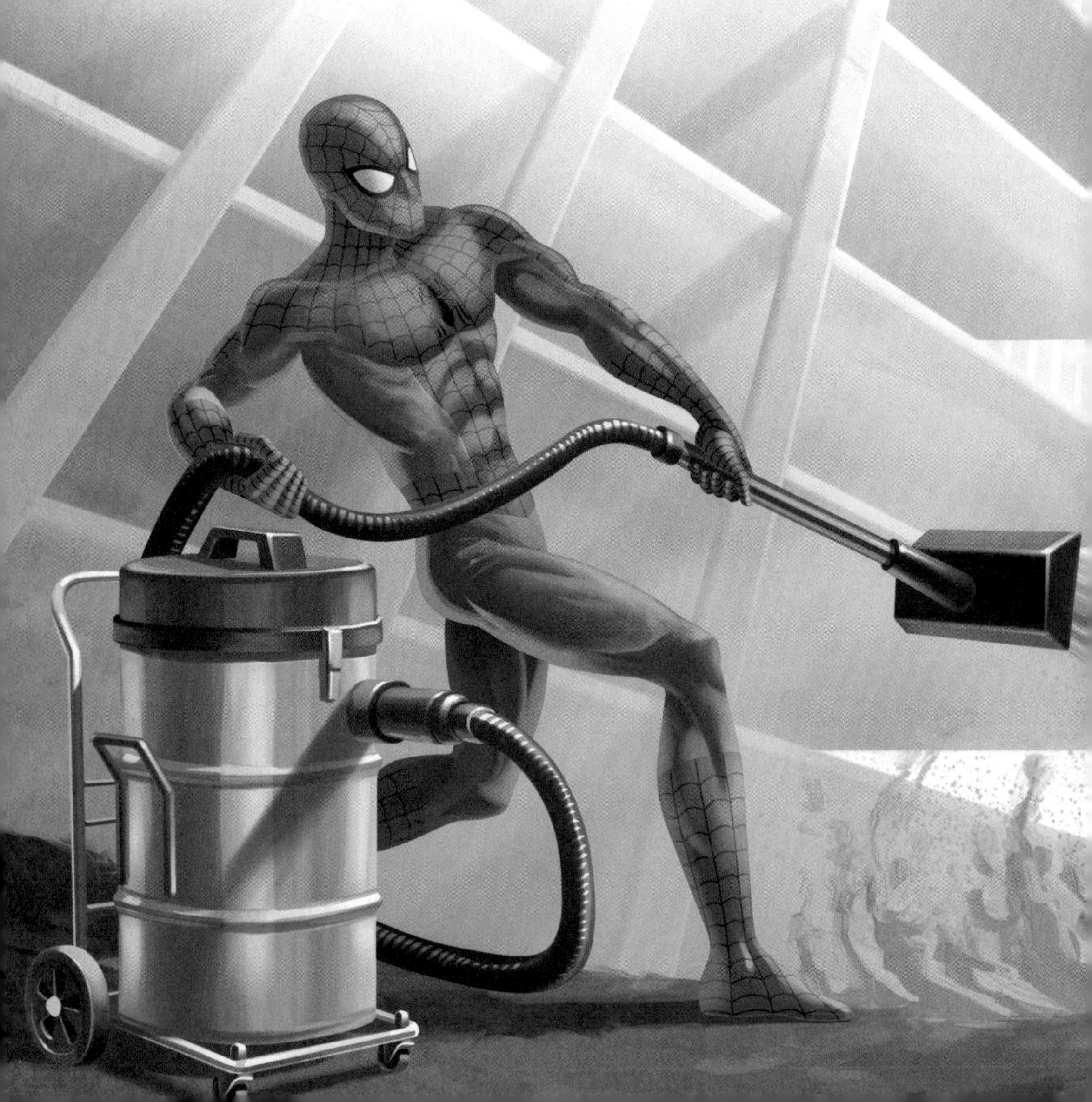

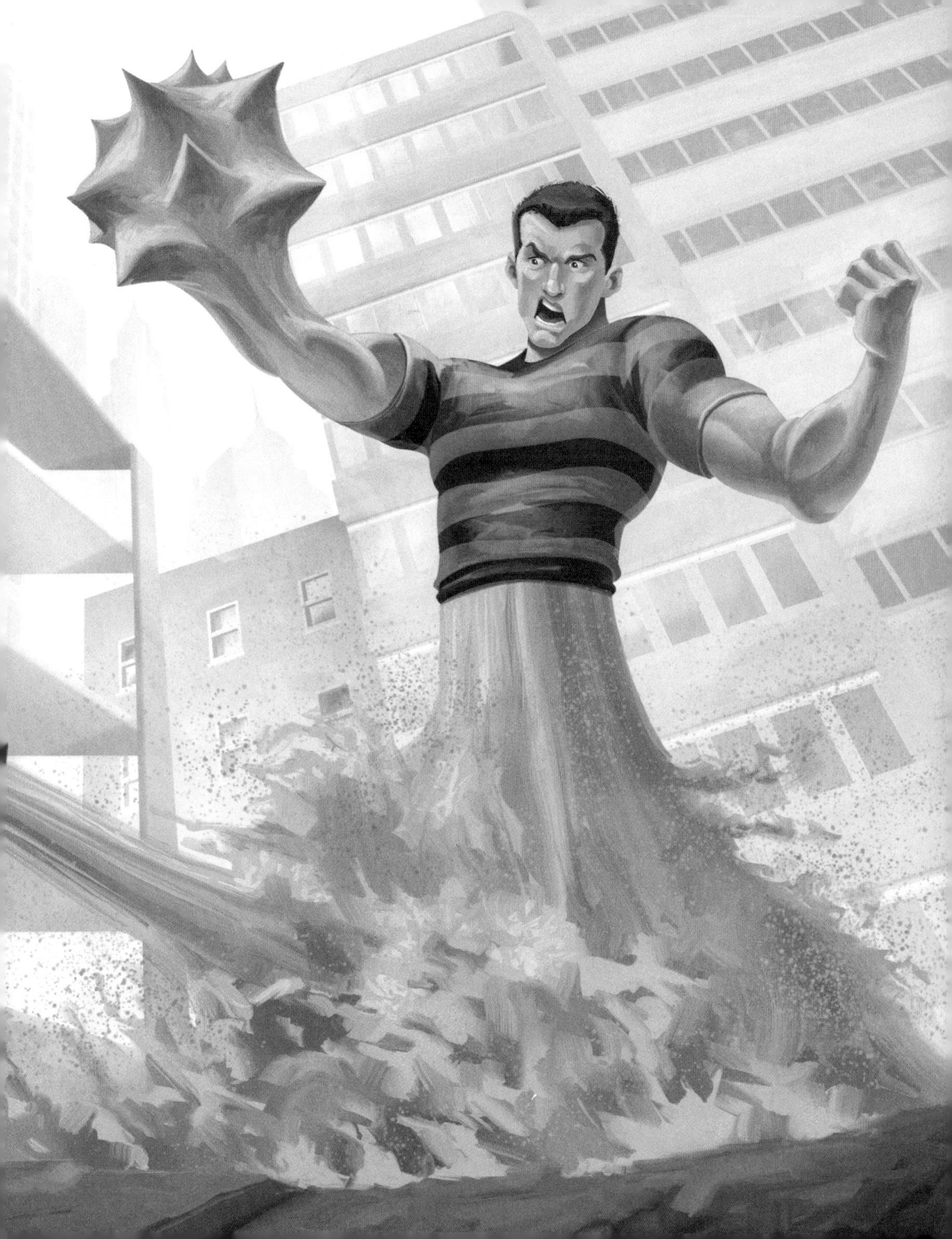

The Lizard was once a doctor—but his research with lizards turned him into a half-man, half-reptile monster. Spider-Man needs all his amazing powers to escape the Lizard's whipping tail and sharp claws!

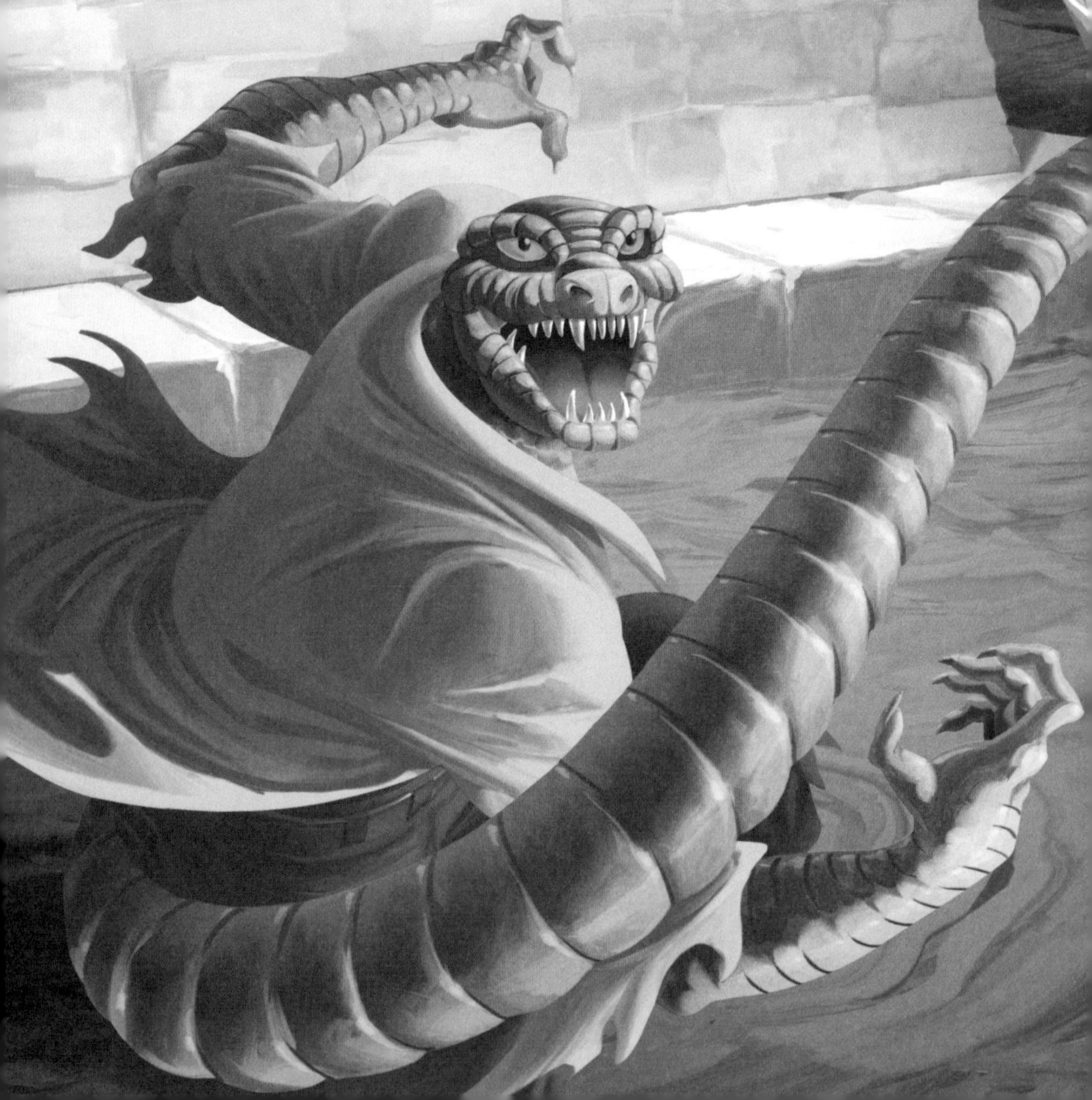

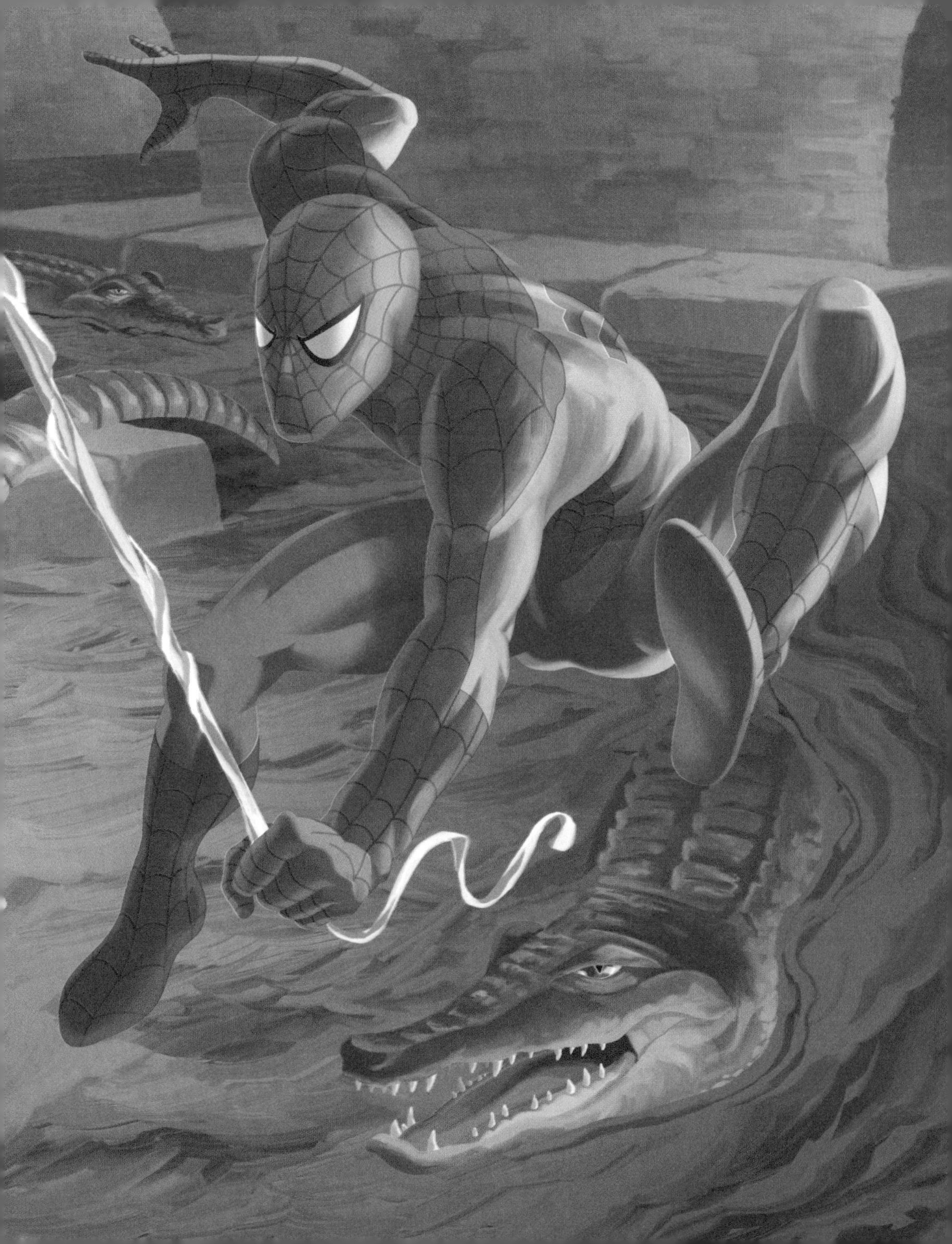

The Green Goblin commits crimes with a rocket-powered glider and a bag full of explosive pumpkin bombs. The Goblin's gloves can fire powerful electric shocks, so Spider-Man has to move fast when he faces this frightful fiend!

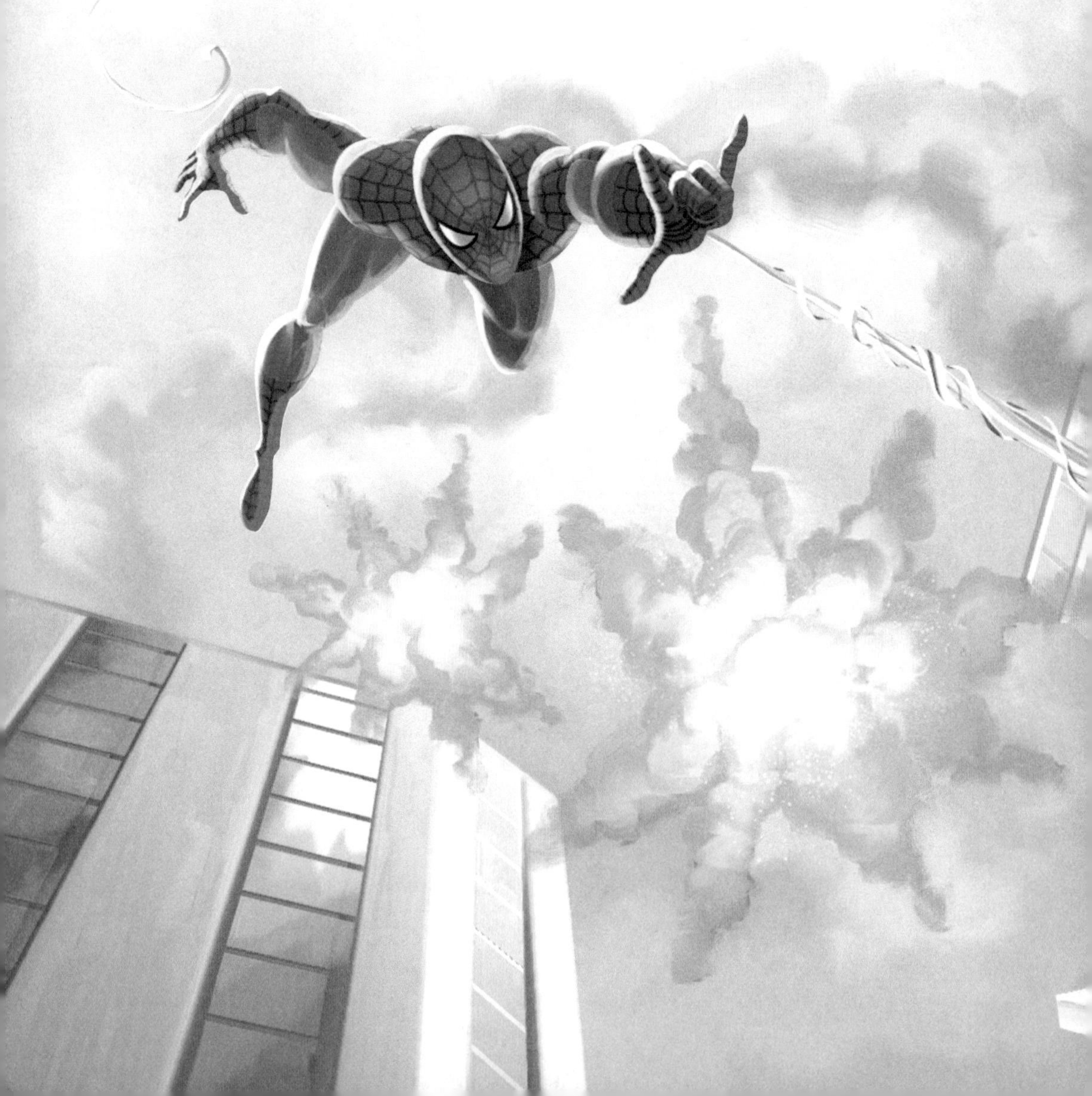

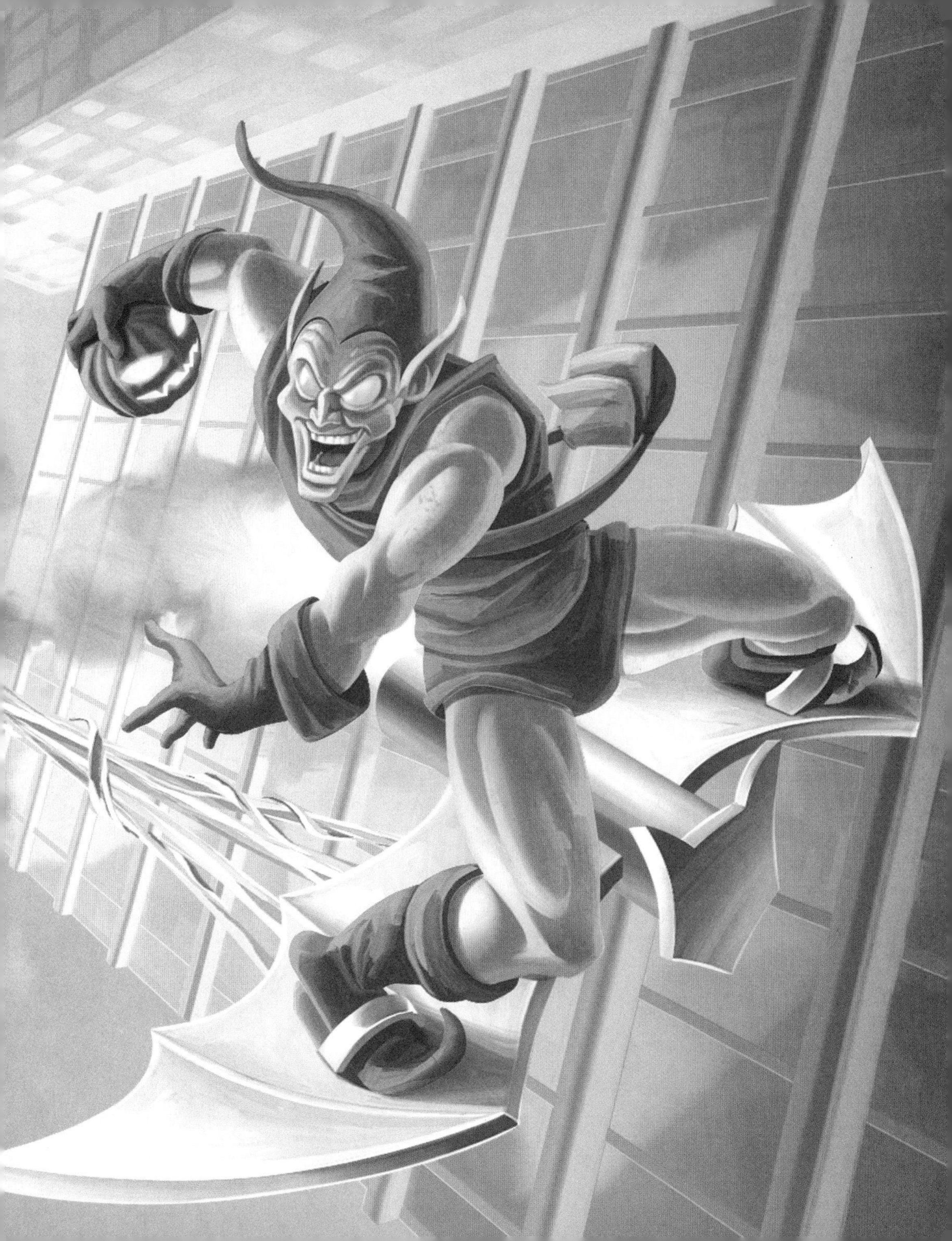

The world is a much safer place because Spidey keeps on swinging.

Go, Spider-Man!

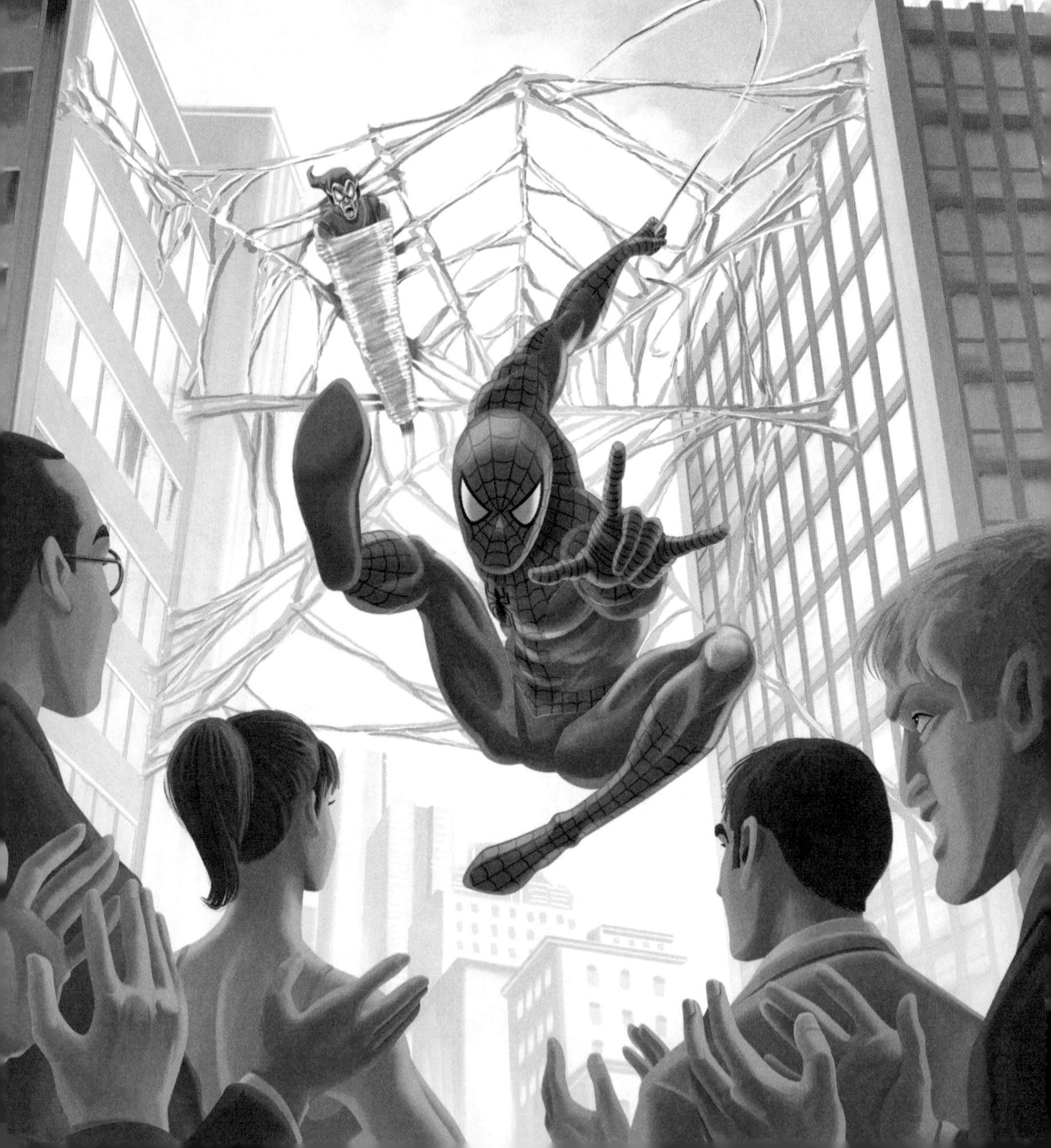